FARM OF THE DEAD THINGS

A Dead Things Story

Ryan M. Williams

GLITTERING THRONG PRESS | RAINIER WA

Glittering Throng Press
PO BOX 179 RAINIER WA 98576-0179

glitteringthrongpress.com

eBook ISBN-13 978-1-946440-45-7
Paperback ISBN-13 978-1-946440-46-4

GTP No : 13

CONTENTS

CHAPTER I

T HE STORY MUST BE told, that's as true today as it was back on that Friday in 1968, when Stefan Roland, Craig Marshal and Noah Crane filmed dead things rising from their graves.

The air was heavy, hot, and still when Stefan popped open the van door and slid out onto the gravel beside the road. The on-screen personality of the group, Stefan possessed the casual handsomeness of an old western sheriff, crossed with a more modern relaxed professional style. From his mop top haircut and his neat, close-trimmed beard, to the long cut of his jacket, and dark sunglasses, he looked every inch the up and coming television news reporter. Out of the van he pulled off his sunglasses and surveyed the isolated road. Nothing in view except for the low stone fence along the edge of the graveyard with yellow and brown leaves piled up against the stone. The place looked worse for the wear with a couple sections crumbling down. Two deep puddles filled the ruts leading up to the modest wrought iron gates. And it was quiet. He didn't even hear any birds or crickets. Not even frogs and this late in the day there should be frogs croaking in some nearby pond. Beside him the side door of the van slid open and Crane came on out.

Also young, Crane fit the hippy ideal from his sandals to his beads and tie-dyed shirt. His ginger hair spread out around his head in a mass of curls, the unfortunate result of his attempt at an Afro. He whistled softly. "Wow, man. Look at this place."

"Right." Stefan turned back to the van. "Marshal —"

The dude in question slid on out of the van holding onto his camera. He wore thin jeans and a bright orange cardigan, and like Crane, sandals. He let the camera hang by the strap from his shoulder as he climbed down.

"Yeah, boss?" Marshal asked.

Stefan gestured at the empty road and the old cemetery. "Is this the right place? It doesn't look like anyone gets out here. Man, this place is dead."

Crane laughed. "Good one."

Stefan shook his head. "Look, I wasn't trying to crack a joke, but I think someone is trying to pull something over on us."

"Dunno, man." Marshal shrugged with one shoulder. "The man I talked to said that someone had been messing with graves here. Springwood Cemetery, just like the sign says."

"And I thought you said that the Inquisition was investigating?" Stefan pointed his sunglasses at the closed gate. "I don't see anything that looks like the Inquisition."

"Dunno what to tell you. I only know what the man said."

"Hey man," Crane said. "We're here. Let's check it out. If we don't shoot something the station is never gonna pay up for the trip out here. All we got to do is get in and get a shot of you in front of a disturbed grave, right? Grave robbing is news, right?"

"Yeah, right," Stefan agreed. "Assuming we find anything disturbed."

"Not a problem." Crane laughed. "I'm sure we can scuff up some grave if we need to."

"Nice idea," Marshal said.

"Hey! It's not my fault that we came all the way out here and there ain't nothing going on, is it?" Crane turned to Stefan. "Is it, man? I didn't even want to come on this joy ride."

"No, man. It isn't your fault. Fine. Let's see what we can find. Maybe the man you talked to is around here some place. Either way, get your gear together. If we can find the guy I might be able to get something on film, but I'll tell you man, this doesn't look like my big break."

Stefan left Crane and Marshal to gather the film and sound equipment while he checked out the driveway leading up to the cemetery. Gravel and dried leaves crunched beneath his black leather wingtips. The quiet started to bother him. He grew up in the city and out here away from the busyness and excitement of the city he felt cut off. Much like he felt cut off from the career he'd imagined he'd have. He detoured around the big puddles in the ruts leading to the gate, and the grass-covered ground along the sides of the drive squished beneath his shoes. He grimaced and went on around to the firm ground on the other side. Up close the gate wasn't locked, only shut. He still didn't think it was worth the risk of getting the van stuck to drive it up through the puddles. Stefan lifted up the heavy iron hook that held the gate shut and gave the gate a shove. The hinges squealed like an angry cat but the gate swung open a couple feet. Back at the van Crane and Marshal were untangling cords. Stefan left them to sort it out and stepped on through the gate.

More puddle-filled ruts dotted the dirt lane as it ran out into the cemetery. On either side marched ranks of headstones, statues and grave markers. Big old maple trees dotted the cemetery, the leaves on some starting to turn yellow while others looked untouched. The sun hung low in the sky behind one of the larger trees. Stefan slipped his sunglasses back on and walked on up the driveway on the lookout for the man Marshal had talked to about the disturbances. He didn't see the man but something did catch his eye, the cemetery sloped up away from the road, and several rows up fresh dirt marred the green lawn. Stefan rubbed his beard and looked back down the drive. Crane and Marshal had gotten the gear sorted out and were starting toward him, skirting the puddles on the drive. Stefan raised a hand and waved.

Marshal waved back. Stefan pointed up the slope and got a nod back in return. *Good enough. Let the guys catch up when they could.* He wanted to see what was up there. He set off through the grass, which obviously hadn't been mowed in a while. It rose up higher than his shoes and quickly wet his feet. He ignored it and walked around the nearest headstones.

The closer he got the clearer the dirt area became. A grave with a weathered headstone at the top, but the ground was all churned up like someone had dug it up and then put everything back. There were chunks of sod all uneven like a patch of broken ice on a pond. Something had obviously disturbed the grave, very recently too, because the piles of dirt didn't show any sign of having been worn down by the recent rain showers that had made the puddles on the drive. Stefan looked back down the drive. Crane and Marshal had started up the slope toward him, he beckoned to them. "Up here!"

His encouragement didn't speed up their pace at all. Stefan turned back to the grave at his feet. This grave did look like it had been disturbed, which fit what Marshal had been told. Small town grave robbing? Or a prank by the kids at the university? Hard to say. And without an interview with a caretaker or local sheriff it wasn't going to be much of a story. Stefan looked at the headstone.

Albert Thompson. Loving Husband, Father and Grandfather. 1878 - 1959.

Family, that'd be another angle. If they could track down Albert's family and interview them about the disturbed grave, that might add the human element he needed. Turn this into a real story. A glint in the dirt caught Stefan's eye. He bent down and brushed away moist dirt clods. A worm wiggled beneath the dirt but that wasn't what he had seen. A bit of gold metal caught the sunlight and glowed with bright reflections. Stefan brushed a bit more dirt away revealing what looked like part of a segmented gold watch band. He picked up a dirt clog and dropped it back over the part he had uncovered. It looked pretty much like how he'd first seen it and would make a good shot on camera when he uncovered it. They'd also need a shot with him in front of the cemetery gates to set it all up.

Crane and Marshal made it up to the grave.

"Whoa, man," Crane said. "What happened here?"

Marshal hoisted his camera up to his shoulder. "This is what the man said, the caretaker guy. He's keeps finding graves all messed up like this."

"Okay, here's what we're going to do," Stefan said. "I'll do a piece here by the grave. There's a watch there in the dirt —"

"Where?" Crane bent to look at the grave.

"Never mind it right now. Get the sound set up. We'll do the piece and I want Marshal to film me finding the watch. We'll take in the headstone and then we can take a look around and see if we can turn up this caretaker. When we go I want a piece in front of the gates. If we can't find the caretaker we can try talking to the local sheriff or look up this guy's family."

"It's already getting late," Marshal said. "We're going to lose the light soon."

"Then let's get this thing done." Stefan positioned himself beside the grave. He buttoned his jacket. "How do I look?"

"Cool, boss." Crane got his microphone up. "Okay, I'll record when you give the word."

"Ready," Marshal said.

"Okay. Three, two one." Stefan put on his serious, concerned face. "I'm standing at the side of one of these disturbed graves, a plot belonging to the late Albert Thompson. As you can see, the grave has been dug up very recently."

Stefan turned, keeping his profile in the shot and looked down at the grave. He brought his hand up and stroked his beard. "Well, look at this. I see something in the dirt there."

He bent down and brushed away the clog of dirt that he had placed over the watch band. "It looks like a gold band, maybe a watch." He dug a finger into the moist soil and dragged it out of the ground. A man's watch, sure enough, caked in dirt. It dangled from his finger catching the evening light.

"A man's watch, maybe belonging to the late Mr. Thompson. We'll make every effort to return this to the man's family." Stefan pulled a handkerchief out of his pocket and made a show of wrapping the watch before he slid it into his pocket. He waited for a count of two. "That's a cut."

"Are you really going to give that watch back?" Crane asked.

Stefan didn't bother answering. "Let's look around and see if we can find this caretaker. I'd really like to get him in on this since he called us. We could use some local color. There must be some sort of caretaker's shack or something, right?"

"Dunno," Crane said.

"Come on." Stefan set off back down the hill toward the road, trusting the others to follow.

Marshal kept his camera up on his shoulder. "I'm going to get some background shots in case we need them."

"Great," Stefan said without slowing.

He walked down the rows of graves with Crane on his heels. Marshal lingered and wandered away from them as he got the background shots he wanted. Stefan had nearly reached the road when he noticed a man up ahead, off to the side of the road, walking toward Marshal. The man staggered and caught himself on one of the headstones. He was, oddly enough, wearing a tux, but it looked rumpled and dirty even at this distance. Stefan pointed out the man to Crane.

"Do you think that could be the caretaker?"

"In a tux?"

"I don't know, he looks like he has been roughed up." Stefan started toward the man. "We'd better see if he needs any help."

"It'd make a better story if he got roughed up trying to stop the dudes that messed up the graves."

Stefan didn't bother answering. He hurried through the wet grass toward the man. He raised his hand when he got closer. "Hey there."

Marshal was still closer to the man than Stefan and had his camera up, filming Stefan's approach. The man looked at Stefan but then shambled on toward Marshal. Stefan heard him making a noise, like a growl deep in his throat.

"Excuse me, are you the caretaker?"

The man ignored him and kept heading toward Marshal. Marshal actually started walking backward to keep the shot.

The man in the tux moaned. Stefan put on more speed. He jogged up behind the man. "Excuse me, we're from channel five news. Can we have a word, please? About what has been going on here?"

Then the wind shifted and Stefan caught a whiff of something harsh and chemical, and the smell of rotten meat. The odor caused his throat to clench and his gorge to do somersaults. Slowly the man turned to face him with clouded gray eyes. He sniffed heavily at the area and then let out the most mournful moan as he stared toward Stefan. The man's skin was sunken, dried out and looked too pale. Stefan twirled his hand in the air.

"Film this!"

"I'm filming," Marshal answered.

Stefan watched the man warily, holding out his hands. "Now calm down. Can you tell us what has been going on here?"

All he got in response was a low groan and the man lunged at him with out-stretched hands. His fingernails were torn, the ends of his fingers in tatters and oozed a foul dark fluid through the caked dirt. Stefan's stomach turned over, and he took a couple steps back to keep the distance between them.

"No hold on there..." Stefan shook his head. He looked right at the camera. "He's dead, man."

CHAPTER 2

T HEN DEAD THING CAME at Stefan again,
grabbing at his jacket. Stefan's jaw tightened, and he
grabbed the dead thing's arms and shoved it away. Still
groaning the dead thing came back at him. Stefan didn't
back away this time. He grabbed its arm and swung it
around as if they were at a square dance, and then let go.
The dead thing stumbled back, tripped and fell. The back
of his head hit the sharp corner of a grave marker with a
sound like a melon hit with a hammer. His feet kicked
against the wet grass for a second, and then he lay still.

For several seconds none of the men moved.

"Whoa," Crane said, breaking the silence.

Stefan made a chopping motion with his hand. "Cut.
Stop filming."

Marshal shut off the camera and lowered it from his
shoulder. "Is he dead?"

Stefan took a couple steps back toward the body. It
hadn't moved since it fell. The eyes stared vacantly at the
sky. "Man, he was already dead, just a dead thing."

"But he was walking and making noise," Crane said.

"Yeah." Stefan tasted bile in his mouth. "Yeah, but he was dead anyway. I mean look at the guy. All covered in dirt, his clothes and hands all messed up. Look at his fingers!"

They all gathered around the body.

"So what do we do, boss?" Crane asked. "I mean, are people going to believe us?"

Stefan shook his head. "We'll cover our bases." He brushed the dirt from his sleeves and looked at Marshal. "Let's shoot again. Another segment. Start on me and pull back when I signal."

"What?"

Stefan position himself beside the body. He made a rolling motion with his hand. "Come on, let's get this. Then we'll do the piece by the gate on our way out of this dump."

Marshal lifted the camera into position. "Ready."

"Three, two, one. We've made a grisly discovery." Stefan paused for a breath and continued. "Grave robbers have desecrated this quiet Springwood cemetery. While searching for the caretaker we discovered that the robbers didn't get far with their stolen body."

Stefan signaled with a flick of his fingers. He gave Marshal a second to pull back and include the body in the shot. Stefan pressed his hands together into a prayer position. "Although we cannot confirm at this time that this body is the remains of Albert Thompson it seems likely to this reporter. Final confirmation will need to come from the county coroner."

A two count and Stefan said, "Cut. How'd that look?"

"Great," Marshal said. "But man, we've got film of this dude walking around."

"And I'm telling you that the guy was already dead when he was walking around." When Marshal shook his head Stefan stepped past the body and grabbed Marshal's arm. "Don't believe me? Then touch him. Go on! He's cold. I felt it when I wrestled with him. And the way he felt — he's just a dead thing."

Marshal slung his camera and went to the body. Stefan crossed his arms and waited. Marshal looked back up at them both. Gingerly he reached out and touched the neck. He jerked his hand away as if shocked. He got back up in a hurry.

"That's why the guy said the Inquisition was investigating," Crane said, excitedly. "It wasn't because of grave robbing, it was this weird shit."

"Maybe," Stefan said. "Come on. Let's get the gate shot before it gets too late."

"You're going to leave him here?" Marshal indicated the body.

Crane laughed. "What're you gonna do with him, man?"

"I don't know, it seems weird."

Stefan shook his head. "We leave it all for the sheriff or the Inquisition. Right now I want to get that gate shot and then see what else we can find out. For one, are there more of these dead things walking around?"

"Okay, man." Marshal started backing away from the body. "Let's go then."

"Totally," Crane said.

Together they left the body and headed back to the road. They hadn't gone far when Stefan saw something crawling through the grass alongside the road ahead. He held up a hand. "Just a sec. I see something. Marshal?"

Marshal got the camera up on his shoulder. Crane turned on the sound gear. Stefan went on ahead. He looked back at the camera. "We see something up ahead, alongside the road. Not sure what it is, but we're going to take a look." He got closer and the dark shape let out an loud caterwaul that raised goose bumps on his arms and stopped him in his tracks. "It sounds like an animal in pain."

Stefan took a couple more careful steps and the shape in the grass crawled up onto the road. It was a cat, but it also another dead thing. One back leg hung by nothing more than a strip of flesh. Half an ear was missing, and the eye and most of the skin on the left side. The cat's once white fur was caked with mud and patches had fallen away. It tottered out onto the dirt driveway and yowled again.

"Holy crap," Crane muttered.

Stefan kept his distance but beckoned to Marshal. "Get a shot of this. Folks at home, this is a terrible sight. This cat is in awful shape. It looks dead, but it's on its feet and making that noise. I can't even begin to describe the smell of it, but I'm sure you can imagine it isn't nice."

The cat lurched in Stefan's direction. It hissed and growled deep in its chest. He took a step back. "It seems understandably agitated. I think we'll keep our distance and let the proper authorities deal with the poor animal."

Stefan backed away across the road to circle around the cat. Crane and Marshal followed him.

Then Marshal said, "Boss, look!"

Marshal had the camera pointed back up the slope of the graveyard. Stefan turned around and saw what Marshal had seen. Two more people in the graveyard, a woman and a man. The man was too far away to see clearly but the woman was wearing nothing but mud and dirt. She staggered through the graveyard toward them. The man also walked with an odd, unsteady gait. The cat yowled again.

"At this point I think it is best we leave and let the authorities and the Inquisition deal with this situation." The cat crawled unsteadily in their direction, still growling. Stefan twirled his hand. "Keep filming, Marshal. We're going to want all of the footage, but let's get back to the van."

Together they set off back down the road to the gate at a fast pace. Not running, the dead things were slow and aimless in their movements, but Stefan didn't want to risk getting too close again.

"Do you think it's a witch behind this?" Crane asked as the gate came into sight.

"I don't know, man," Stefan said. "But I'll tell you this, there's definitely a story here and we're going to get it on film. All of it."

"What about the Inquisition?"

"We haven't even seen them. And if they do show it I think it's about time we got them on film. Don't you?"

"Sure, I guess so. But they might not like it."

By that point the gate was just ahead but Stefan saw another dead thing shambling down the slope in their direction. He touched Marshal's arm and pointed out the newcomer. "I don't care, people have a right to know what's going on."

A fly buzzed around Stefan's head. He swatted at it and kept going all the way to the gate. He slipped through and waited for the others to get through then he pulled it shut and dropped down the latched with a dull clang. He positioned himself in front of the gate.

"Okay, let's get the setup shot now. Ready?"

A quick count, Crane nodded, and Marshal gave Stefan a thumbs up. "This is Stefan Roland, reporting at

Springwood Cemetery where we've received news of disturbed graves and the possibility of an investigation by the Inquisition. It raises the question, is there witchcraft at work?"

Stefan paused and the said, "Cut. How was that?"

"Um, boss?" Crane nodded at the cemetery.

Stefan turned and looked. Two of the dead things had reached the dirt lane leading through the cemetery and were coming toward the gate. "Right. Let's get in the van and go back down the road. Not too far. I want to stay on this and see what they do."

They all got into the van, Stefan behind the wheel so that the other two could film and record what was happening outside. He put the van into reverse and backed out of the drive into the road and then down the road another hundred feet or so. Marshal leaned out the window with the camera.

"How's that?"

"I've got a clear shot of the gate. Let's wait here."

Stefan put the van in neutral and let out the clutch. He leaned on the wheel, watching the graveyard. "Do you realize this might be the first time anyone has documented an event like this?"

"That's assuming that the Inquisition doesn't confiscate our gear, man," Crane said.

"They don't have the authority."

Marshal didn't look away from the camera, but he spoke up. "Are you kidding? They're like the feds on steroids. They go wherever they want, any country they want. If they decide to take our gear I'm handing it over."

Stefan shook his head. "If it comes to that you give me the camera. I'll deal with them. Something like this could be good for them, build up their image."

"And yours," Crane said.

Stefan looked in the back where Crane lounged against the seat. "Look man, this could be big for all of us. You saw those dead things back there. There hasn't been a modern event like this, and we're right here in the heart of it. I just wish we could talk to that caretaker guy that called, find out some things."

Marshal tapped his shoulder. "Hey look, guys. They're at the gate."

Stefan leaned forward to get a better look. Two of the dead things stood at the gate. The naked woman and some guy in a suit. They reached out and pushed at the gate. Even from here he heard the gate clanking and a low moaning noise. A third figure shuffled into view, it looked like a man in blue jeans and a flannel shirt, with the right side of his neck a bloody ruin. The blood had gone all down his shirt and pants. He joined the others in grabbing the gate, but he shuffled along the bars, shoving past the others to get at the center. He fumbled at the latch.

Stefan's breath caught. He had to get in the shot on this, the moment when the dead things were getting out of the cemetery. He spun in his seat and opened the door.

"What're you doing, man?" Crane called from the back.

Stefan ran around the front of the van, the hot air stale in his mouth. He skidded to a stop on the road in Marshal's shot. He looked back and then took one step to the right. "Come on, let's get this. Crane!"

Crane slid open the side door and stuck out his mic. "Fine. Ready."

"What you see behind me should disturb everyone. Those aren't people trying to get out of the cemetery, but zombies." Stefan took a breath and looked back at the cemetery gate. The dead thing in the flannel shirt was pawing at the latch. He lifted it and it dropped back in place, but for how long? Stefan turned back to the camera. "That's right, zombies. Dead things brought back to a semblance of life. There have been other cases in history, but none so recent as this, and none with a trained news crew on site. We are sticking to this story to see how it develops.

"Right now the cemetery gate holds the zombies back, but for how long?" Stefan took another look. Two more figures approached the gate, and he heard the sound of the cat's caterwaul on the wind. "We also don't know what supernatural force animates these creatures, but traditionally they are associated with a single twisted personality, one equipped with the supernatural ability to raise the dead. If that's the case here we haven't seen any sign of the witch behind this."

Stefan heard a loud clank and turned to see the dead things had managed to unlatch the gate. They kept pushing and the heavy gates swung open with metal squealing. Stefan pointed at the zombies.

"Here they come! It's a terrifying sight, the dead literally risen from their graves and they're coming out now into the street itself and there's no sign of anyone here. No local law enforcement, no sign of the Inquisition, we're alone out here on this street. There aren't any houses close by…" The dead things finally noticed Stefan and the van down the street. Blank eyes turned to face them. Stefan held his ground a moment longer. "We are going to stay with this story, to bring you the truth behind what is happening here, but we can't let them get too close. We'll back off and see what they do."

With that Stefan hurried back around the van to the driver's side and got in. Marshal kept the camera on the zombies shuffling out onto the street. With Stefan out of sight now in the van the zombies lost their focus. They stopped where they stood, one man standing up to his ankles in one of the puddles in front of the gates.

"There are more of them now," Marshal said softly.

CHAPTER 3

S TEFAN SAW THAT HIS cameraman was right. Past the gates more dead things shuffled toward the open gate. In the small slice he could see there had to be at least a half-dozen more moving.

"Crane —"

Crane waved his hand. "Quiet, man. I hear something."

In the back seat Crane held his microphone pointed out the partially open side door. He adjusted the controls and touched his fingers to his headphones. "I can't make out what that is."

Stefan listened carefully. Distantly he heard the moans of the zombies. The dead cat yowled again. A couple flies flew in the open window and buzzed about battering themselves against the front windshield. Then he heard more buzzing and saw more flies outside.

"Close the window! Shut that door!"

Crane pulled back his microphone and shoved the door closed, but not before several more flies flew in through the gap. Marshal pulled the camera in and started rolling up the window. A few more flies slipped in before he finished. The cloud of them flew around the van buzzing. Stefan grabbed the morning paper that he had stashed between the seats and swatted at the flies. Outside a dark cloud of flies flew past and around the van. They landed all over the windows, obscuring the view.

"What the hell?" Crane asked.

Stefan shoved the paper back down beside the seat. "Hang on."

He pushed in the clutch, shifted into reverse and slowly started to back up the van. At first the flies on the windows and mirrors didn't do anything. He gave the van more gas, trying to see where he was going as best he could, but the flies made it difficult. He went a bit faster and then suddenly the flies all took off. He braked and shifted back to neutral. They'd gone another few hundred feet down the road. The flies outside flew in a dark cloud toward the cemetery which continued to spew out more zombies that shuffled aimlessly around the drive in front of the cemetery with a few wandering near the road. Without prompting Marshal had already rolled down the window and was filming the scene again.

"Look man," Crane pointed at the dash.

Stefan saw that the flies which had flown into the van lay dead on the dash. A couple had fallen to the floor beneath the dash. Marshal turned the camera and took a shot of the dead flies scattered across the dash.

"What killed them, do you think, boss?" Crane asked.

Stefan looked at the flies, and back to Crane, knowing that Marshal was still filming. "Maybe they were already dead, and when we backed up we took them out of the range of the witch, or whatever is causing this? I don't know but if that is true it suggests a limit to the affected area."

"But why flies?" Crane asked. "That's just gross."

Stefan shook his head. "I don't know, man. But flies must die all the time, right? Seems like it to me, anyway."

Marshal turned the camera back to the view outside. Stefan saw dark shapes flying above the cemetery. *Birds? More dead things?* The haze in the air had to come from the flies and other dead insects. Whatever was happening, it clearly wasn't limited to the people in the graves. Every dead thing was getting up and moving, and they were getting it all on film. This was going to be huge but he wanted to know the answer to the question the audience was asking. *Why?*

For the moment they all sat and watched the dead things gathering around the cemetery like watching storm clouds growing on the horizon. After a few minutes Stefan heard the sound of a car approaching and checked his mirrors. A dark sedan was coming down the road toward them at high speed.

"Come on guys, let's get out and see who this is." Stefan opened his door without waiting for an answer. Behind him he heard the sliding door open, and the passenger door. Stefan shut his door and walked around to the front of the van, just in case whoever it was didn't stop. Crane and Marshal took up positions behind him, and it made him feel better that everything was being filmed. Even from this point he could hear the zombies groaning and other odd cries and noises from the graveyard. A shadow flitted across the road. Stefan looked up and saw a flock of crows or black birds flying toward the cemetery.

The sedan pulled on past the van, turned across the road and stopped blocking both lanes. Front and rear doors opened and men got out. Sharp red suits with thin black ties and polished black shoes. All of them wore large dark sunglasses, all were white with their hair slicked back.

"It's the Inquisition, man," Crane whispered.

Stefan beckoned to his crew and started walking toward the inquisitors. "I'm Stefan Roland, reporting on this developing situation. We're happy you're here."

One of the inquisitors, tall with sandy blond hair, came forward, unbuttoning his jacket. Stefan caught a glimpse of a gun on the inquisitor's hip.

"You're reporters?" The inquisitor asked.

"That's right. We were called about disturbances at the Springwood cemetery. Can you shed any light on what is happening here?"

"For your own safety we need you to leave," the inquisitor said. "This is an Inquisition matter now. Get back in your vehicle and go."

Stefan shook his head. "People need to know about this. We have an obligation to stay."

The inquisitor didn't move. One of the others came close and whispered something. The inquisitor nodded. "If you don't leave now we will arrest you for interfering in this operation and adding and abetting a witch."

"So there is a witch involved here?" Stefan pressed.

"Get back in your vehicle now."

Stefan held up his hands. "Okay, man. We're going." He headed back to the van. Marshal and Crane made it there first and climbed in.

Once inside Stefan put the van in gear and swung it in a wide turn across the road. He bumped down off the side of the road and then back up onto the asphalt and headed in the opposite direction. Marshal lowered his camera.

"Is that it? Are we done?"

Stefan laughed and shook his head. "Hardly. We're going to check out the roads on the other side of the cemetery and see if they have it all blocked off."

"Should we do that, boss? What if they do arrest us?"

Stefan shrugged. "They can arrest me if they want." He glanced over at Marshal. "How're we doing on film?"

"We're good, man. No problem."

"Great. Because is big, you know? We can do this like a whole feature, not just some segment. We get the station to back it and it could go nationwide. People need to see this."

Up ahead Stefan saw the dirt road that ran off east on his left. No sign of any other cars. He took the turn and increased his speed despite the rough conditions. Marshal got up and crawled between the front seats into the back of the van. He went to the window behind the driver's seat and had the camera ready. A farmer's field stretched away on their left toward the cemetery, which was a dark tree line in the distance.

Glancing out his window Stefan thought he saw something like a haze hanging above the cemetery, a sort of swirling disturbance. *Flies? Bugs? Birds?* He needed to get around to the other side.

At last they came to another road running north and south, paved but cracked and obviously little used. Stefan turned back toward the cemetery and gunned it. His mouth felt dry as he sped down the road at nearly fifty miles per hour. Was the Inquisition ahead of them on this road, more zombies or both? It didn't take long before he had his answer.

Dead things were massing outside the cemetery, but not the Inquisition. Those zombies that had come out the gate on the other side were the minority. Stefan licked his lips and brought the van to a crawl.

"Damn," Crane said.

Marshal had the camera at the window. "Look at them all."

A crowd of dead things spilled out of the cemetery onto the long hillside between the cemetery wall and the road, but they weren't just standing there. Most lurched, shuffled, staggered and even crawled north, along the cemetery fence.

"Man, where are they going?"

"I don't know," Stefan said. "Let's find out."

"I'm not going to get as good of a picture through this window," Marshal said.

"I can fix that." Stefan swung the van across the road, shifted and then backed up into the road again to put the sliding door on the side facing the zombies. Marshal reacted immediately, climbing across Crane to open the sliding door. Crane shrank back from the opening. Several flies immediately flew into the van.

"You're crazy!"

"Get the gear ready," Stefan ordered. When Crane didn't move Stefan gave the van more gas. They picked up speed backing down the road toward the zombies.

Crane swore and got the microphone ready and pointed the dish out the door.

Through the open door Stefan had a clear view of the dead things. Most of the human dead things looked long dead, like mummies in their best dress but here and there among them were fresher zombies. There was a young woman who even looked pretty at first glance with a long sleek black dress, blond hair tumbling in curls past her pale unmarred shoulder but when she turned her head the right side of her face was a dark ruin of torn and mangled flesh still weeping bright blood. She looked right at them with clear eyes and bared her bloodied teeth.

Stefan kept the van moving. Marshal and Crane kept recording. A few zombies had wandered down to the road but not many, he thought he could get around them. Just then the dead young woman growled and shoved aside a withered old granny zombie. The girl zombie started running at the van. Stefan noticed her feet were bare but bite marks and blood marked her left leg and foot beneath the dress. Had she been a mourner at the cemetery when these things clawed their way out of the graves?

"Boss?" Crane asked, his voice anxious.

She picked up speed. Sprinting down the grass at them. Not at all slow like the rest. Stefan gave the van more gas, accelerating in reverse down the road. The girl zombie altered her direction, still coming on fast. More dead things noticed and turned toward the van. A group ahead started coming toward the road. Dead voices groaned as they came at the van.

"Faster, boss," Crane urged. "She's coming fast!"

He gave the van more gas but the distance between the open side door and the dead girl had already halved. She was about twenty feet away, running fast down the slope.

He heard her panting as she sprinted at the van.

He was so busy watching her that he didn't see the dead guy coming up the road at the van until the last second.

He turned the wheel, trying to swerve around the guy, but the corner of the van clipped the zombie and knocked him aside. Crane yelled and caught the door to prevent himself from falling out. Only ten feet between the van and the running zombie, with at least a dozen more zombies coming behind her as fast as they could manage.

Stefan floored the pedal. The van picked up speed. Enough at the last second that she came up short, with her hands grasping at Marshal, her growling pants filling the van, but she didn't quite reach the door. Her fingernails scratched alongside the passenger door, and then he was past her. She staggered out into the road in front of the van. Then she recovered and her eyes locked on his. He didn't see any intelligence there, only hunger. She ran after the van. Stefan smelled rot and decay on the wind coming in through the door.

He looked back, watching the road. More zombies stood closer to the road, turning as the van approached. He kept going in reverse as fast as he could to get past them and still give Marshal the chance to make the shot of the crowd of dead things moving away from the cemetery, human and otherwise. The air looked thick with insects and birds. He saw smaller shapes squirming through the grass. It looked like every corpse, no matter how small or large had risen up and all of it was on the move, heading north.

The van cleared the zombies crowding the road. Stefan glanced back the way they'd come, but then girl zombie had slowed. She was still coming but not running. He let off the gas and brought the van to a stop, shifted back to first and pulled across the road to give Marshal another shot of the oncoming dead things.

More and more dead things turned their empty gaze toward the van. The dead girl led the pack, not yet running but walking quickly down the road in their direction. Marshal kept filming. The cries of the dead things grew louder and more flies flew into the van. Crane cried out and swatted at the flies. The distance between them and the gathering dead things shrank further. Stefan heard the sound of the dead girl panting. Her pace picked up to an unsteady jogging when she was maybe thirty feet away. Behind her came even more zombies and the general direction of the crowd started turning toward the road.

Crane's hand beat the back of Stefan's seat like a wounded fluttering at a window. He had dumped the recording equipment on the seat, still running.

"Come on, man! Let's go!"

Stefan ignored him. The gap between them and the girl shrank more. Twenty feet. Fifteen.

"Roland!" Crane yelled shrill, and panicked as he lunged for the sliding door handle.

CHAPTER 4

T HE DEAD GIRL PUT on a burst of speed and in seconds was less than ten feet away. Crane shoved the door but Marshal put out a hand and stopped the door, holding it open with the camera in the gap. Crane shoved on the door handle.

"Come on, man! She's right fucking there!"

And she was right fucking there, reaching out with scratched and bloodied nails to grab at Marshal but the camera man yanked the door closed in the last second. Her nails scrambled at the side of the van, trying to get at the handle. Marshal flipped the lock and raised the camera to the window. She attacked the window, her once pretty face bloodied and torn up. She bit and clawed at the glass. More zombies were coming behind her. Stefan put the van in gear and pulled away from the dead things.

"Bye baby," he said.

Marshal cracked up. He fell back in the aisle in front of the back seat and laughed and laughed. Stefan laughed too, he couldn't help it. He glanced back and saw Crane crouched up on the seat looking at them both with wide eyes. His face looked drained of blood. Stefan checked the mirrors. The girl zombie wasn't running after them. The whole crowd of dead things continued to stagger along the road in this direction, the air thick with things that flew, and smaller shapes crawling and lurching through the grass. He didn't see any sign of the inquisitors. He eased off the gas and kept the speed low enough to stay ahead of the dead things without leaving them behind.

Marshal finally stopped laughing and got up, climbing back into the front passenger seat. He dropped into the seat with a sigh and set the camera gear on the floor. "Man, that's some fucked up shit back there. What do you think is going on? Where are they all going?"

"Beats me," Stefan answered. "But we're going to find out."

"They would have torn us apart if they got in here," Crane complained. "Why don't we take what we have and get out of here?"

Marshal shook his head. "No way, man. And next time why don't you try doing your job instead of panicking?"

"Screw you!"

"Hey, guys!" Stefan interrupted. "Let's not, okay? Something caused all of this. We've got to get to the bottom of it, and then show everyone. That's what we do. I said it before, but this is our big break. You dig? If we keep it together, stay cool, man, we'll write our own ticket."

"I just don't need him telling me how to do my job."

Stefan shot Marshal a look before the cameraman could say anything. "Fine. For now, let's stay ahead of them and see if we can figure out where they are going."

The van crawled down the road at no more than ten miles per hour to stay ahead of the dead things.

Stefan kept an eye on them in the mirror. On either side of the road were brown fields bordered by trees. Up on the right stood a collection of buildings, white farm house, a long low barn with a rusted metal roof, a round silo, and a paddock dotted with black and white cows. The farm was a good distance from the road, unless the dead things changed their course they'd go right past the farm. Marshal took the camera and crawled into the back of the van to shoot out the rear hatch.

As he'd thought, the zombies didn't turn away from the road to approach the farm house. If anything more of them drifted away from the road to the ditches and fields on the left side. When they came to a fence they walked into it, fell over it, or pushed through it but kept going. Some stuck to the road and just kept coming. They were about a mile past the cemetery now, all the dead things keeping more or less in a group, when Stefan saw headlights fast approaching. He hadn't even realized how far the sun had sunk until that moment. He switched on his own headlights and honked his horn to get the driver's attention.

Whoever was behind the wheel, they didn't slow. The car shot past them, a dark Cadillac, headed straight toward the zombies and other dead things. Stefan hit the brakes and came to a fast stop. He twisted around.

"Are they stopping?"

"Not yet," Marshal said.

Stefan shifted the van into reverse and headed back down the road after the car. A couple seconds later the car was close enough to the zombies in the street for the headlights to light them up. The brake lights came on. The zombies didn't waste any time shambling to the car. The dead girl, still leading the pack on the road, ran right up to the caddy and grabbed at the door. This time she got lucky and managed to get a good grip on the door handle, popping the driver's side door open.

Stefan's stomach clenched, and he gave the van more gas. He honked the horn as he reversed, trying to get the zombies' attention. Nothing had any effect. Faster than he would have expected more than a dozen zombies had surrounded the car. It looked like they were trying to climb into the driver's side. Stefan couldn't make out exactly what was happening. Marshal had the camera up and was filming but Crane just sat on the back seat like a lump.

"Crane! We need to record this!"

Crane stirred, looked out the back with his face bleak. "You can't be serious."

"Do it," Stefan said. "You said you didn't need anyone to tell you how to do your job? Well, then get to it!"

The zombies had someone, the driver of the caddy, and pulled her out into the street. Her screams cut through the night. She wore a pale pants suit, stained in splotches of red. Her blood. Stefan stopped the van. He couldn't get any closer without risking the same thing happening to them. He grabbed the door handle and his hand shook. He shoved open the door and jumped down. There was a crowd of zombies in the field, more around the car with the woman, still screaming and fighting back against the zombies. She shoved the dead girl away into the others. For a second the space around her was clear.

Stefan ran past the rear of the van but more zombies came around the caddy and surrounded her again. He rubbed his jaw and backed away from the mob. He looked at Marshal and realized he was on camera.

"This is horrible," he managed to say. "We tried to get the driver's attention, but she didn't stop and then the dead things closed around her so fast!"

The zombies weren't alone in the attack. A cloud of flies flew around the zombies and several dark birds darted into the fray and away again. Crane threw up, leaning out the rear hatch, but he kept the microphone pointed in more or less the right direction. Stefan's own gut clenched when the woman's screams stopped.

"We saw the inquisitors back on the other road past the cemetery, but none since. Maybe if they'd been here this terrible tragedy could have been prevented, if they had up road blocks or anything but we're alone out here."

Moans from the zombies carried on the wind. The activity near the car diminished. Several of the zombies turned their attention back down the road. Stefan saw more and more dead eyes turning in his direction. He took a step away. Just then the crowd parted. He saw the dead girl that had chased him, and beside her on the ground was the driver. Clearly dead. Her pants suit ripped open, along with her insides. Zombies shoved bits of gore into their bloodied mouths as they shambled in his direction. The dead girl gobbled down a chunk of unidentifiable flesh and then reached out a hand as if pointing at him. Marking him as next.

Stefan took another step back and looked at the camera. "Clearly they've noticed our presence. I wish we could have done more, but we've got to get moving to stay ahead of them."

The driver's foot twitched. Stefan didn't move.

The woman groaned loudly and rolled onto her side but the zombies didn't pay any attention to her.

He felt a chill settle over his limbs when he realized why. She'd become one of them. Dead birds clustered on the top of the car took off, screeching their disappointment. She pressed her bloody hands onto the road and slowly climbed to her feet. It looked like someone had taken a giant ice-cream scoop out of her stomach. Her once pale pants suit was mostly covered in red and darker stains. Her blond hair clung wet and red to her skull. One eye socket was empty, trailing gore down her cheek. With her remaining eye she looked straight at Stefan.

The weight of that gaze was like an accusation. It compelled him to move. He backed up almost to the van's bumper, out of view of the camera. His mouth felt dry. He turned, staggered as if dead himself, and ran back for the driver's side door.

Loud groans rose up in the darkening twilight behind him. He reached the door and his heart lurched when a hefty figure stepped into the beam of the headlights wearing a decaying suit. Zombies from the main group had come over to the road. More stumbled down into the drainage ditch. Something flew past his head carrying with it the reek of rot and decay.

Stefan pulled open the door and looked back along the van. Crane started yelling. The dead girl and her recent victim both growled and ran at the van.

Marshal wasn't playing chicken this time. Stefan heard the rear hatch drop. He jumped in and slammed his own door closed. The zombie in the front of the van came around the bumper toward the driver's side door. He shifted into gear and hit the gas. The van lurched and for a second he thought he had killed it by popping the clutch too fast but it caught and the engine revved as they shot ahead. The van bumped the zombie by the front of the van, knocking him away.

No other zombies in the road, but a bunch beside the road as he pulled away. Stefan accelerated quickly, shifting gears until he reached forty miles per hour. Only when the dead were nearly swallowed by the darkness did he finally ease off the gas.

"You guys okay back there?"

"I think I shit myself," Crane said.

"I don't know if we can show this footage," Marshal said. "That woman's family might object."

Stefan's heart still thudded in his chest, but he shook his head. "People got to know about this, man. We can't cover it up."

"I hear you, but they might not let us."

No need to mention who they were, the station executives or the Inquisition or federal agents. There were plenty of people that might squash this before it got out.

But the idea made Stefan feel sick. A fly buzzed by his face. He swatted at it.

"No. We've got to find a way, but first we need to know why this is happening."

"How are we going to find out?" Marshal asked.

Stefan looked in his mirrors. He couldn't see anything behind them. He hit the brakes.

"What're you doing?" Crane cried.

"Waiting. The only way we're going to find out what is going on is if we see where these dead things are going."

"We don't know that they're going anywhere," Crane objected.

"They're all going in the same direction. It isn't like they've scattered in every direction. They're going somewhere and I'll bet it has something to do with what is going on."

CHAPTER 5

A SHORT DISTANCE AHEAD on the left side of the road, Stefan saw lights just past some small Douglas fir trees. From what he could see it looked like a trailer. He tapped the window. "We need to warn those folks about what's coming."

It wasn't far. Stefan pulled into the dirt driveway, lights flashing across a rusted swing set with blue and white spiral limbs, a bicycle discarded on a weedy lawn and two dented aluminum trash cans beside the wood porch. Marshal crawled up from the back.

"Think they'll let us use their john?"

"You'd want to go in a dump like this?" Crane asked. "Who knows what you'd catch?"

Stefan ignored them and got out. He heard the sliding door open too, so evidently the guys were getting out as well. He headed straight for the front door, mostly straight except when he had to avoid stepping in piles of dog crap, and hurried up the wooden steps. He knocked hard on the metal frame of the screen door, rattling it. A dog started barking inside the trailer and first a woman's voice, then a man's hollered at it to shut the fuck up. A second later the main door was yanked open by a stringy woman wrapped in a blue terry cloth robe with pink curlers in her hair. A half-smoked cigarette dangled from her lips. The lines around her eyes deepened as she looked at him.

"Who the hell are you?" Her eyes shifted and she pointed a bony, liver-spotted hand. "And who the hell are they? What're you doing with that camera?"

Stefan glanced back, not surprised to see Marshal filming the scene while Crane recorded. He looked back to the woman. "I'm Stefan Roland, ma'am. That's my film crew. There's something strange going on, and I need you to listen carefully."

"This is some trick, isn't it?"

"No ma'am." She scowled but Stefan hurried on. "I know how implausible —"

"What?"

"How unlikely this will sound, but we've just come from Springwood cemetery. The dead people there have risen from their graves, along with every other dead bug, bird and animal in the area and they're coming this way."

She didn't move for a couple seconds as if his words had frozen in where she stood. Then she hollered so loud that Stefan nearly jumped back.

"Earl! You gotta hear this! This man here says that judgment day has come!"

From somewhere in the trailer the dog started barking again and the man shouted at it and her to be quiet.

"It isn't judgment day, but the dead are coming. We saw them kill a woman only a little way up the road. You and your husband need to get in your car and get out of here."

She shook her head. "Car's all busted up. Don't run worth shit."

"We've got room in our van, but we have to go."

She took a long drag on her cigarette and blew smoke at the screen door. Stefan coughed, and she shut the trailer door in his face. He banged on the door frame again.

The woman hollered from inside. "I got my twelve gauge here!"

"I hear them," Crane said.

Stefan turned around. Crane had his microphone pointed back the way they'd come. He turned back to the door and banged on it with his fist. The door flew open, and he found himself looking at the black barrels of a shotgun through the screen.

"See?" The woman said around her cigarette, still dangling from her lips. Smoke curled out of her nose. "Now get the hell off my property."

Stefan took a step back, holding up his hands. "We're only trying to help. They are coming."

"Anyone else shows up here I'll show them the business end of this." The shotgun twitched in her hands. "I don't think you're moving fast enough mister. Get!"

"We're going." Stefan made his way down the steps. He waved at the others, and they retreated back to the van.

The woman stepped back and let the door swing shut. Stefan hurried back to the van. Once inside he started it up. So far he didn't see any of the zombies. He backed out into the road. It was getting too dark to see far behind him.

"How far back do you think?"

"Not far enough," Crane said.

Stefan let the van idle. They still had a half tank of gas. Enough for now. He rolled down his window. The wind whispered in the trees, chilly as it blew into the van. Even from this distance he heard the dog barking in the trailer and the wordless, futile shouts of the people.

He gripped the wheel until his knuckles turned white. *Why wouldn't they listen?* Sure, it sounded crazy, but still, sticking a gun in his face?

"Boss, what're you doing?" Crane asked.

"Waiting." Stefan leaned on the window. He closed his eyes and listened. Then, faintly, he heard them. Low groans and moans in the distance, the harsh cries of the birds in the dark sky and beneath it the persistent buzz of the dead flies. The sound floated on the wind and raised goose bumps on his arms. He twisted around.

"Get back to the hatch. I'm going to pull forward enough so you have a shot of the trailer. Tell me when to stop."

Crane rubbed his face and his cheeks looked wet. Marshal just crawled into the back, dragging along the camera gear. He popped the rear hatch and pushed it up. The wind felt cold on Stefan's neck. He put the van in gear and moved it slowly forward.

"That's good," Marshal called. "Crane, come on."

"Damn you both," Crane said. Still, he picked up his equipment and joined Marshal in the back.

Stefan left his window down and waited.

It didn't seem that long before the first shadows appeared out of the night, flying around the brightly lit windows. Then a zombie walked out of the night into the yard. It was the unfortunate woman that hadn't stopped her caddy. Right behind her came others, and he saw hints of movement around the sides and back of the trailer. The dead things converged on the trailer and even the dog fell silent.

Stefan watched carefully, but for the moment he didn't see any dead things nearby except he heard flies buzzing about.

The caddy driver reached the porch steps first. She started up, tripped and crawled the rest of the way. Once on the porch she pulled herself up on the screen door. The trailer door flew open and the woman was there again, a dark shape against the light.

"Lord in heaven!" She cried.

The shotgun blast cut through the moans and cries of the zombies. The caddy driver's body flipped away from the porch and fell into darkness, but more zombies came at the door. The woman backed up as they ripped apart the screen. Screams joined the moans of the dead.

Stefan looked away.

He stared at the dash for several seconds. The dog started barking again, and he looked back at the trailer. Zombies crowded all around it, hitting it with their hands. The whole thing rocked on its blocks. A line of them led to the open door. Then zombies fell away and the dog, a big black dog ran out of the trailer, knocking aside zombies in its way. Stefan leaned out the window and whistled sharply.

He couldn't see the dog in the dark, but he leaned across the front of the van and opened the passenger door. A zombie appeared in the doorway, a balding man with skin peeling away from his skull. Withered hands reached into the van.

CHAPTER 6

CRANE SCREAMED IN THE back. Stefan swung around and kicked at the zombie, hitting it in the head. It stumbled back and a large dark shape jumped up into the van.

It was the dog, a massive brute with hanging folds and big drooping eyes. Stefan leaned across the dog and pulled the door shut. The zombie he had kicked returned and beat at the window. Stefan hit the lock and moved back into his seat. The dog jumped up in the passenger seat and bared its teeth at the zombie.

He heard the rear hatch shut and looked back to find the camera aimed at him. Marshal gave him a thumbs up. Crane had his face in his hands, but he didn't look hurt. Stefan turned forward and realized that there was a face right at his window.

The dead girl from the cemetery stood right outside his window looking at him. The dog barked, the sound deafening in the van. Stefan hit the gas and the van jumped forward. Dead fingers grabbed at his door and slipped away.

A couple other zombies staggered around the road but Stefan swerved around them and kept going.

"Can we go home now?" Crane asked.

Stefan didn't answer, but if he found a connection back to a highway or something he was tempted to take it. The dog sat placidly in the passenger seat, panting softly. With the road ahead clear Stefan rolled up the window with one hand while he held the wheel with the other. Up ahead a bright red reflector caught the headlights on the side of the road. He slowed but the reflector only marked what looked like a dirt road or driveway leading off into the darkness. He kept going.

A minute later the headlights caught something ahead. More zombies, out in the roadway, coming toward the van. Stefan slowed to a stop. Marshal came up between the seats with the camera.

"How'd they get in front of us?"

"I don't know." Stefan didn't see that they had many options. The crowd ahead looked too thick. The dog growled deep in his chest like an engine at work. "This has to be a different group, no way they got ahead of us."

Crane laughed in the back. "That's just swell."

"We'll have to go back to that turn off we passed a minute ago. There's nothing else unless we try to force our way through them."

"There are more behind us," Crane said.

"So we'd better get to the turn off first." The zombies ahead were getting close. The dog barked once. Stefan shifted into reverse and backed up until he had enough room to turn around. Soon they were driving back down the road. Another reflector marked the turn off from this direction as well, Stefan turned and took it.

The road or drive had grass growing down the center and the tracks were like a washboard. The van rattled slowly along with the headlights lighting up the field ahead. A dark hill with a few trees and a white, slat-wall farmhouse at the top rose up ahead. As near as he could tell the road was taking them to that house. A dim light lit up one of the windows, so someone must be home.

The driveway turned a corner and headed more directly toward the hill.

"Wait," Marshal said. "Back up."

"Why?" Crane asked from the back.

Stefan didn't question it. He stopped and put the van in reverse. As he backed up the lights shone out into the field. Then he saw it. Dark shapes moving through the field on two legs. More zombies, but headed toward the house on the hill.

"This is where they're all going," Marshal said.

Crane laughed. "Oh that's fucking great. We're right at the middle of all of this?"

"Hang on," Stefan said.

He started driving on up the road, faster now. The van bounced over pot holes. It was risky, but he didn't want to be cut off either. Even if the zombies and other dead things were coming to this house they might be able to hold them off. And if the dead things were coming here there might be a reason. Like the person responsible.

"Have the gear ready. When we get out I want you to be filming and recording everything."

"Is that all?" Crane asked.

"Yes!" Stefan looked in the rearview mirror. "That's all man! Hold the microphone. Record what happens so that people know what went on here tonight. Okay!"

"Why not?" Crane asked miserably.

The driveway curved around the hill and came up the backside. As they rounded the last curve the headlights caught more dead things down that side of the hill. This place was the bulls-eye and they'd been herded right to it by trying to stay ahead of the dead things from the Springwood cemetery.

It wasn't much of a house. A rectangular farmhouse, white paint gone gray with age and weather, peeling off the slats in places. Moss covered much of the roof but through yellow curtains light glowed in one window on the first floor. Back behind the house on one side was a sagging old barn and paddocks with broken fences. A rusty old pickup with side-boards sat alongside the house.

Stefan parked the van behind the pickup and got out. The dog followed him, Marshal and Crane got out the sliding door with their equipment. Marshal had the camera's spotlight on now. Stefan faced them, the house behind him.

"Ready? Three, two, one." Stefan took a deep breath. The light from the camera was blinding, but he looked to the side at the dark night.

Overhead he heard the birds cry out. "The dead things we've followed tonight are coming here, to this isolated farmhouse. We've encountered groups of them coming from all directions. They're here now, and we're going into this house to see if there are any answers or refuge from the dead."

Stefan walked up the cracked and weedy concrete walkway to the front door. He knocked on the dark blue-painted wood. Like the rest of the house it had seen better days and the paint was a web of cracks now. Marshal's light lit up the whole doorway. Stefan raised his hand and knocked again. He heard boards creaking inside.

A woman in a gigantic pink spotted dress opened the door. Stringy hair hung down in her face, she was tall, an inch or two taller than Stefan and large. Her frame filled the doorway. She looked at Stefan, her face expressionless.

"I expect you're here about them dead things?"

"Yes, ma'am, you know that they are coming here?"

She heaved a big sigh. "You'd best come in before they do get here." The corners of her mouth twitched as if she might smile. "Unless you want to stay out there."

"Thank you, we'll come in."

She moved on into the house. Stefan followed with the dog at his heels, and then the guys with the gear.

Crane closed the door after they were in and turned the dead bolt. She led them into a small living room past the stairs. Two other doorways in one corner. A couch slowly decayed on one side of the room while a dusty television sat on the opposite side, on with the evening news playing. A smell of fried chicken and sour milk hung in the air. In front of the couch was a small glass-topped coffee table with three KFC buckets on the top. A few flies buzzed around the buckets.

The woman moved past the coffee table and dropped onto the couch, which sagged so much that it looked like it might fold up around her. She reached into the middle bucket and took out a drumstick. The dog sat down at one end of the coffee table and watched her intently.

There wasn't any place other than the couch to sit. Stefan went around the other side of the coffee table and perched on the padded arm of the couch. "My name is Stefan Roland, I'm a reporter. These other men are my crew and the dog, well, he joined us when the dead things attacked his owners."

She bit into the drumstick and didn't say anything. She tore loose a long strip of greasy meat with her teeth and then tossed it to the dog. It landed limply on the floor. The dog looked at it, then back to her and didn't touch the scrap. She shrugged. "Suit yourself."

"Could you tell me your name?"

She still didn't look at him, just stared at the television. "Might as well, I suppose. I'd have thought folks like you would turn up sooner than this. I've been waiting." She gestured at the television. "So far there's been nothing."

"We've been filming," Stefan said. "When we get back we'll be able to report."

She nodded. "That makes sense. I'm Glenda Barker. It was me that woke those dead things. I've got the gift."

"Why?"

She chewed on the drumstick, slurping the meat off the bone. As she chewed, she answered. "When it started I didn't mean to, it just happened. Little things at first. A mouse caught in a trap, or a spider I'd squashed. Kinda fun once I got the hang of it."

"You said you woke them, how could you do that? Are you a witch?"

Glenda chewed at the scraps on the bone. When she finished she tossed it into the right hand bucket. "I don't know about that, it's a gift, that's all. A sign from the Lord that I'm blessed. I can raise the dead just as surely as Jesus raised Lazarus! It's time people knew that, paid me a little respect."

Something hit a window at the back of the house. The dog growled.

"If you woke them, can you make them go back? Can you stop them?"

Glenda reached into the center bucket and pulled out a wing. "Why? With them to do what I want?"

Another thud against the house. Stefan heard moans from outside. If she couldn't stop them it sounded like they would break in soon.

"Why are they coming here?"

"Because I woke them. They know who I am, and when you all show your film so will everyone else. I'll be rich! Can't you see it? Everyone will want their dead back, and I can give them that."

"These dead things have attacked and killed people."

Glenda bit into the wing and chewed off the meat. She sucked the last slivers free and tossed the wing into the right hand bucket again. She closed her eyes and for a second Stefan thought that she was falling asleep but then the bucket on the right shook. He heard snapping noises from inside.

Several more blows hit the windows, all around the house. The moans grew louder.

Then the bucket tipped over and greasy bones tumbled out onto the table, scattering apart. Then the bones rolled and snapped and reconnected again into the shape of a bird without feet or a head. It flopped off the table and fell apart again.

The dog whined. Glenda opened her eyes and chuckled.

Something pounded on the door.

"Glenda, you need to stop them, before they break in here," Stefan said.

"Don't you tell me what to do! No one tells me what to do!"

Stefan rose up off the couch. "I'm not telling you, I just wonder if you can do it."

Glenda's head fell forward, her hair hiding her face. She reached into the bucket for another piece of chicken.

CHAPTER 7

S TEFAN BECKONED TO THE guys, and they followed him over to the other doorways. One led to the kitchen, and at the back, another door. Stefan leaned into the other. It smelled like dirty gym socks, but he could make out a bed, and a door at the end. *A bathroom?*

"Come on." They all, including the dog, followed him into Glenda Barker's bedroom. As he walked past a dresser he noticed something. "Marshal, bring your light over here."

The light pointed at the dresser. There was a scrapbook on one side of the dresser. Stefan picked it up and went on around the bed, past a closet to the other doorway. Sure enough it led into a bathroom.

"Okay. We'll hole up in here. We can push the dresser over in front of the doorway, pull it into place from the inside and close the door. There's only that one small window above the tub. I don't think the dead things will get in."

Something hit the window above the bed and elsewhere in the house Stefan heard glass break. "Come on!"

Stefan snapped his fingers at the dog and pointed at the bathroom. It obediently ran inside. "Crane, help me with the dresser."

Marshal went on into the bathroom. Together Crane and Stefan shoved the dresser over in front of the doorway, leaving only a gap to squeeze through. Then from the inside they pulled it over completely in front of the door. Stefan shoved the door closed.

The space was pretty small and it smelled of piss and mold. Dark stains crawled along the ceiling and walls. A stand-alone sink with a cabinet beneath it, a toilet across from that and the tub along the wall. The dog jumped into the tub. Marshal put down the toilet seat and sat down, the camera still running. Crane perched on the edge of the sink and Stefan leaned back against the door.

The house echoed with the bangs and thumps from the dead things. The moaning cries carried through the walls.

"How long do we wait in here?" Crane asked.

Stefan shook his head. "As long as we have to, until those things go away or the Inquisition shows up and gets rid of them."

"You think that'll happen?"

"They know about it, but I'll bet it was a bigger problem than four inquisitors could handle. They probably needed to get help."

The dog whined and lay down in the tube. Stefan looked at him and shook his head. "He has the right idea."

Marshal shut off the camera and the light, but Crane found a night light in one of the outlets and switched it on. That gave them something to see by. Crane kept recording the sounds of what was going on.

Windows broke. The cries of the dead things grew louder. Glenda started shouting in the other room but soon her shouts turned into screams. Crane took off his headphones and put his hands over his ears, but as loud as she screamed Stefan doubted that Crane could block them out. He felt sick and felt bad when he was relieved that the screams stopped.

"Do you think they'll stop now?" Marshal whispered.

Evidently not. They could still hear the zombies shuffling around the house. Something that sounded like dishes breaking. A cat yowled and it sounded like it came from the bedroom. Wings beat on the bathroom window several times before going away. The dog whined softly in the tub.

Once something hit the dresser, shaking the door, but otherwise nothing tried to get in. Eventually Stefan sat down on the floor with his back against the door. He leaned forward and rested his head on his knees.

CHAPTER 8

T HREE HOURS THEY SAT in the bathroom before they heard the first gunshot. Then more, shot after shot firing. Crane and Marshal joined Stefan on the floor, worried that shots might come through the walls. Several minutes later they heard voices. Stefan gestured at the equipment. He took the scrapbook and shoved it into Marshal's bag. Marshal picked up the camera and started filming.

Stefan heard footsteps in the house. Several more shots, followed by the sound of bodies hitting the floor. Then footsteps in the bedroom and a voice, loudly, "Clear!"

"Help us!" Stefan called out.

That brought shouts and more footsteps. "Hello?"

"We're in here," Stefan said. "Three of us and our dog."

There was a great deal of scraping as the dresser was moved away from the door. Stefan cautiously opened up the door. Flashlights shone in their faces.

Stefan blinked and saw the inquisitor that had spoken to them on the road. He smiled slightly.

"I thought I recognized that van outside. You just couldn't stay away?"

Stefan shook his head. "We had to get the story." Two men in hazard gear carried a body out of the bedroom. It was the dead girl that had chased them from the cemetery. She had a fresh hole in her head, right between the eyes. Stefan looked back at the inquisitor. "I'd like an interview, when you have a moment?"

"I'll have to talk to my superiors about that. Right now we need to get you out of here so that the cleanup teams can do their work. Follow me."

Stefan nodded and led the way out. He whistled and the dog came with him, sticking to his side.

The inquisitor followed them on out of the house and over to their van. A large bonfire burned in the front yard, the smell of singed flesh filling the air.

In addition to the inquisitors' car were three big green national guard trucks and a jeep. Soldiers were active around the house. Two soldiers in hazard gear staggered out of the house with Glenda Barker's ravaged body between them. Like the others she had a bullet hole in her head. Stefan didn't say anything to the inquisitor. The soldiers tossed her body onto the bonfire. She landed on her back, her empty eyes looking out of the flames. Smoke billowed up and obscured her face. Stefan looked over at Marshal and saw that the cameraman had caught the shot.

Gunfire rang out in the night. A soldier with a flamethrower sent fire into the sky, roasting the flies and the birds.

Stefan reached down at patted the dog's head, then crouched. The dog's big tongue licked at his hands. "We'll have to get you a name. How about Buddy?"

The dog leaned against him, his weight almost enough to knock Stefan over. He patted Buddy's back and watched the bonfire burn. He still needed to shoot the wrap-ups, interview anyone he could, find other witnesses and interview them. Then editing and everything else, but he didn't doubt one thing. This film, when they released it, would be big. The career-changing film he'd been looking for.

So why didn't he feel better about it? He'd gotten the story of a lifetime, but he felt sick and empty inside. All he really wanted to do right at that moment was knock back a beer or six and sleep for a week.

Then get back to work.

About the Author

Ryan M. Williams lives a double life as a full-time career librarian and a multi-genre writer with over twenty books. He writes across a range of genres including science fiction, fantasy, paranormal, mystery, horror, and romance. He earned a Master of Arts degree in writing popular fiction from Seton Hill University and a Master of Library and

Information Science from San Jose University. His short fiction has appeared in Pulphouse Fiction Magazine, On Spec Magazine, and anthologies from Pocket Books and WMG Publishing.

To keep up with everything he creates, visit ryanmwilliams.com. Track his many series at their individual sites (FindingDeadThings.com, MoreauSociety.com.) He lives in Washington State with occasional forays into virtual reality.

ABOUT THE AUTHOR

Ryan M. Williams lives a double life as a full-time career librarian and a multi-genre writer with over twenty books. He writes across a range of genres including science fiction, fantasy, paranormal, mystery, horror, and romance. He earned a Master of Arts degree in writing popular fiction from Seton Hill University and a Master of Library and Information Science from San Jose University. His short fiction has appeared in Pulphouse Fiction Magazine, On Spec Magazine, and anthologies from Pocket Books and WMG Publishing.

To keep up with everything he creates, visit ryanmwilliams.com. Track his many series at their individual sites (FindingDeadThings.com, MoreauSociety.com.) He lives in Washington State with occasional forays into virtual reality.

DEAD THINGS SERIES

Waking Dead Things: Book One
Dreaming Dead Things: Book Two
Killing Dead Things: Book Three

Filming Dead Things: A Dead Things Collection